our
Environment

Solar Energy

Kris Hirschmann

KIDHAVEN PRESS
An imprint of Thomson Gale, a part of The Thomson Corporation

Detroit • New York • San Francisco • San Diego • New Haven, Conn.
Waterville, Maine • London • Munich

For more information, contact
KidHaven Press
27500 Drake Rd.
Farmington Hills, MI 48331-3535
Or you can visit our Internet site at http://www.gale.com

LIBRARY OF CONGRESS CATALOGING-IN-PUBLICATION DATA

Hirschmann, Kris, 1967–
   Solar energy / by Kris Hirschmann.
      p. cm. — (Our environment)
   Includes bibliographical references and index.
   ISBN 0-7377-3049-8 (hard cover : alk. paper)
   1. Solar energy—Juvenile literature. I. Title. II. Series.
   TJ810.3.H57 2005
   333.792'3—dc22
                                    2005013356

Printed in the United States of America

contents

Chapter one

What Is Solar Energy?

All day, every day, vast amounts of energy stream outward in all directions from the Sun. This energy is called **solar energy**. Some of this raw power reaches Earth's surface. When it does, it can be used to heat homes and pools, or even to create electricity. Solar energy that has been collected and put to use is called **solar power**.

A Huge Ball of Energy

All of the Sun's energy is made by a process called **nuclear fusion**. Nuclear fusion occurs when the **nuclei** (central parts) of atoms combine. It takes place deep within the Sun's core, where incredible pressure forces atoms together. When the atoms join, they release energy.

The joining of two atoms does not release a lot of energy. But countless trillions of atoms merge every second in the Sun's raging center. The energy created by all these tiny reactions builds up and starts to travel outward from the core. Soon the energy reaches the Sun's fiery surface, where it is released mostly as heat and light. The rays speed off into the cosmos, carrying the Sun's power throughout the solar system and beyond.

In the vastness of space, Earth is just a speck. Most of the Sun's rays miss Earth entirely. But a tiny fraction of the rays—an estimated two-billionths—do find their way to Earth's surface. Two-billionths of the Sun's power may not sound like a lot, but it is actually a huge amount of energy.

The Sun is a fiery star that radiates huge amounts of energy, some of which reaches Earth.

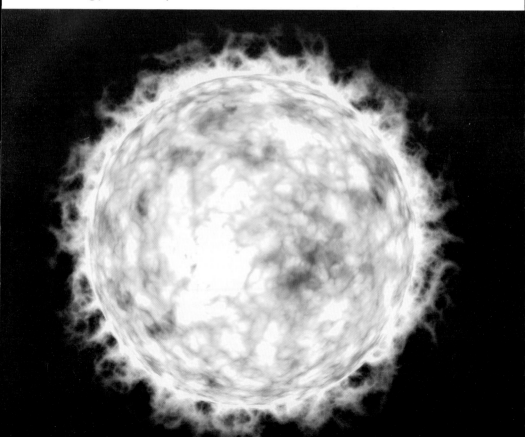

The Sun is the ultimate source of nearly all energy on our planet.

Scientists estimate that the sunlight falling on Earth in one hour is as powerful as all the gas, oil, electricity, and other energy sources used on the planet in an entire year.

Energy on Earth

The Sun's power does much more than just create light and warmth. It also acts as a source of raw energy. The Sun, in fact, is the ultimate source of nearly all energy on Earth, though natural processes may change the energy into different forms.

Wind power is one example of solar energy in a changed form. When the Sun's rays hit Earth, they heat it up, including the air in some places. In other places, such as cloudy areas or regions where it is nighttime, the air stays cooler. When warm air and cool air meet, air currents—also known as wind—are created. Wind power can be captured by devices called windmills. The wind turns blades on the windmills. This motion is then used to pump water or generate electricity.

Hydroelectric power, or power created by the movement of water, also draws its energy from the Sun. When sunlight hits Earth's oceans, some water turns into vapor and escapes into the air. The vapor rises high into the sky, where it may drift for great distances. At some point the water vapor **condenses** and falls back to the ground as rain. Some of the rain falls in high areas, where it feeds mountain streams that eventually become rivers. Hydroelectric dams are built across these rushing rivers to harness the power of the moving water.

Even living beings are vessels for stored sunshine. Plants convert the Sun's rays into food and energy, which are used to build tissue. Animals absorb the tissue—and therefore the stored energy —when they eat either the plants or plant-eating animals. No creature could grow, survive, or even exist in the first place without this energy. It is fair to say that the Sun powers all life on Earth.

Fossil Fuels

Oil, gas, coal, and other **fossil fuels** are yet another type of stored solar energy. These substances began forming hundreds of millions of years ago when plant and animal remains were buried. Chemical reactions, heat, and pressure eventually changed the remains into the forms they hold today. Fossil fuels retain all the energy of their living ancestors. They are like time capsules, holding sunlight from the distant past.

Compared to other energy sources, fossil fuels are fairly simple to collect. Once they are collected, their energy is released by burning. Ease of collection and use makes them cheaper than any other energy source. Humans depend on fossil fuels for this reason. People use gas and oil in their cars, for instance, and they burn coal, oil, and natural gas to heat their homes. Gas and oil are also burned in power plants to create electricity. As a group, fossil fuels today provide about 80 percent of the world's power.

Fossil fuels, however, are a **nonrenewable resource**. This means that people are using up Earth's supply much faster than new supplies can be created. Someday most of the planet's fossil fuels will be gone. Experts disagree sharply about when this will happen, but they are certain that it will happen if people keep using gas, oil, and coal at

Energy in the Earth

Trees, plants, and animals absorb the Sun's energy.

The Sun is the ultimate source of energy.

Remains of trees, plants, and animals become fossils.

Earth crushes the fossils, converting the long-stored Sun's energy into fossil fuels.

the current rate. Scientists are working to develop alternate energy sources that can take the place of fossil fuels.

Energy of the Future

The alternate energy sources that scientists are looking at include nuclear, hydroelectric, wind, geo-thermal, and solar power. Of these, solar power is considered one of the most promising. For one thing, it is **renewable**. This means no matter how much solar energy people collect and convert into power, there will always be plenty more. Also, sunlight is available everywhere on Earth, instead of being concentrated in small areas, like oil or coal. And finally, solar energy is incredibly powerful. All

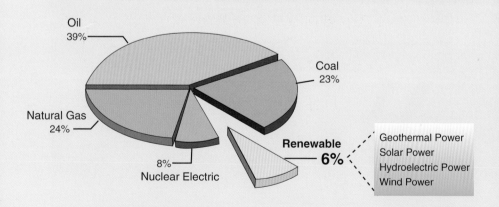

Energy Consumption in the United States

Oil
39%

Coal
23%

Natural Gas
24%

8%
Nuclear Electric

Renewable
6%

Geothermal Power
Solar Power
Hydroelectric Power
Wind Power

Source: U.S. Department of Energy, 2003.

This vast array of solar panels captures and stores the powerful energy found in sunlight.

of the world's power needs could be met with just a fraction of the Sun's energy.

Solar power has another indirect benefit, too: It is virtually pollution free. Manufacturing solar panels and other solar products does produce some pollution. But once a solar power system is installed and operating, it is perfectly clean. Fossil fuels, on the other hand, release sulfur dioxide, nitrogen oxide, carbon dioxide, and other dangerous gases into the air. Any time solar power replaces even a little bit of the energy that comes from fossil fuels, deadly **emissions** decrease.

Unfortunately, capturing solar energy and changing it into usable forms is difficult and expensive. So, solar power is not widely used today. In 2002, solar power supplied less than one-half of 1 percent of the world's energy. Just three countries—Japan, Germany, and the United States—generated about 85 percent of this power. Widespread acceptance of solar power is still a ways off.

Even so, the future looks bright for solar power. Industry experts believe that solar technologies will improve as the years go by, and better technology will lead to cheaper solar power. Fossil fuels, meanwhile, will become more and more expensive as supplies shrink. At some point fossil fuels probably will cost more than solar power does. When this happens, solar power could become a more practical choice for people everywhere. The Sun probably will never supply all of the world's energy. But it seems certain that solar power will be much more important in the future than it is today.

chapter two

Collecting Solar Energy

Solar energy falls freely everywhere on Earth, and it is available to any person who cares to gather it. In its raw form, however, solar energy is nearly useless as a power source. People must use special devices or building techniques to collect sunlight and put it to use.

Solar Heating

Solar heating, or using the Sun's energy to heat homes, is the simplest form of solar technology. Solar heating comes in two forms: **passive** and **active**.

In passive heating systems, homes are specially designed to absorb heat from the Sun's rays. They are made from building materials such as stone and salt-soaked wood, which absorb heat during the daytime and release it throughout the cooler

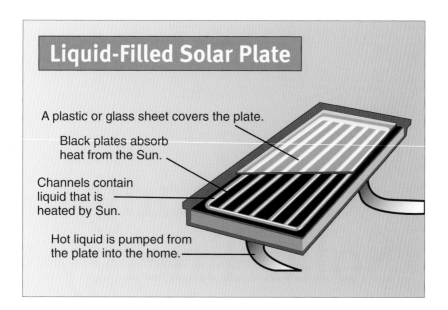

Liquid-Filled Solar Plate

A plastic or glass sheet covers the plate.

Black plates absorb heat from the Sun.

Channels contain liquid that is heated by Sun.

Hot liquid is pumped from the plate into the home.

nighttime hours. Also, sunlight is strongest from certain directions, so every solar home has large windows on its hottest side. In the Northern Hemisphere, solar windows are placed on a home's south side. When the Sun shines, these windows capture energy in the form of heat. At night, the windows are covered so the warmth trapped inside the house will not escape. A house that uses solar-friendly building techniques like these can stay toasty warm on all but the coldest nights.

In active heating systems, mechanical means are used to collect and store solar energy, then deliver it throughout a building. An active heating system usually includes liquid-filled solar plates on the roof. When sunlight hits these plates, it heats the liquid inside. The hot liquid is then pumped through tubes to different parts of the house to provide heat for air or water.

The most effective solar homes include both passive and active design elements. One home of this type is the Impact 2000 House in Brookline, Massachusetts. Built in 1983, this house has roof-mounted heating panels, as well as many passive heating features. The construction of Impact 2000 was featured as a season-long project on the PBS show *This Old House*. The project took place before

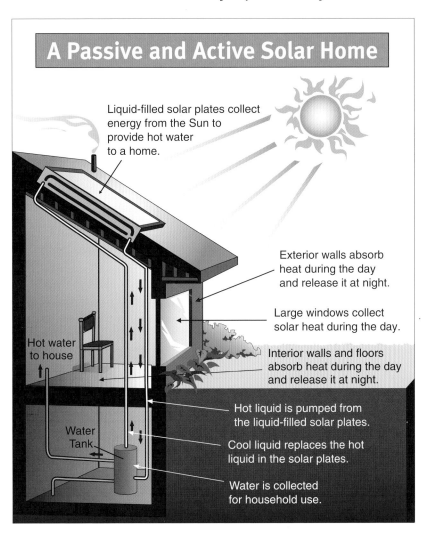

A Passive and Active Solar Home

Liquid-filled solar plates collect energy from the Sun to provide hot water to a home.

Exterior walls absorb heat during the day and release it at night.

Large windows collect solar heat during the day.

Hot water to house

Interior walls and floors absorb heat during the day and release it at night.

Hot liquid is pumped from the liquid-filled solar plates.

Water Tank

Cool liquid replaces the hot liquid in the solar plates.

Water is collected for household use.

solar power was familiar to most people, so it helped educate consumers about the possibilities and benefits of this new energy source.

Even though decades have now passed since the first solar homes hit the market, solar building techniques are still not common in the United States. However, officials are taking steps to encourage people to use solar power. In 2005, for example, California governor Arnold Schwarzenegger unveiled the Million Solar Roofs Initiative (MSRI). Among other things, this plan would require builders to offer solar options to all new-home buyers in the state of California. It would also create a fund to help consumers pay for solar homes. California legislators continued to debate the plan through much of 2005. If this legislation passes, it will provide a major boost to the state's solar-home industry.

Concentrating Solar Power

Another way of putting solar energy to work is to turn it into electricity. **Concentrating solar power** (CSP) devices can do this. In a CSP device, mirrors focus the Sun's rays onto a small area. The focused rays are very intense, sometimes generating temperatures of 7,000°F (3,870°C). They heat a gas or liquid collecting agent, such as melted salt, which is then used to boil water. The steam from the boiling water turns a generator that produces electricity.

The oldest type of CSP device is the **power tower**. In a power tower, a holding tank sits at the top of a tall tower, while a large field of computer-controlled mirrors surrounds the tower and focuses sunlight onto the holding tank. The world's first power tower was Solar One near Barstow, California. Solar One operated from 1981 to 1988. It used more than 1,800 mirrors, each about 20 feet (6m) tall and 20 feet (6m) wide, and produced 10 megawatts of power—enough to supply six thousand people with electricity.

The mirrors on this concentrating solar power device focus the Sun's rays onto a generator found at the device's center.

Another type of CSP device is the **trough system**. Trough systems include row after row of long, curved mirrors. A tube filled with a collecting agent runs along the center of each row. The mirrors reflect sunlight onto the tube, heating the agent inside. In California, trough systems currently supply more than 350 megawatts of power. As of early 2005, another 50-megawatt plant was in the planning stages for an area near Boulder City, Nevada.

The last type of CSP device is the **dish system**. Dish systems use bowl-shaped mirrors, similar to extra-large satellite dishes, to focus the Sun's rays onto a central point. Unlike power towers and trough systems, dish CSP systems do not heat a collecting agent. They reflect sunlight onto a heat-powered engine that generates electricity directly. Dish systems can be grouped together to form a power plant, or they can be used individually for specific tasks. Dish systems are still in the testing stages. When this technology becomes widely available, it is expected to be useful for utility-line backup systems or for bringing small amounts of power to remote areas.

Photovoltaic Devices

Like CSP systems, **photovoltaic** (PV) devices also turn sunlight into electricity, but usually on a much smaller scale. PV devices contain crystals that are "excited" by sunlight. This means that

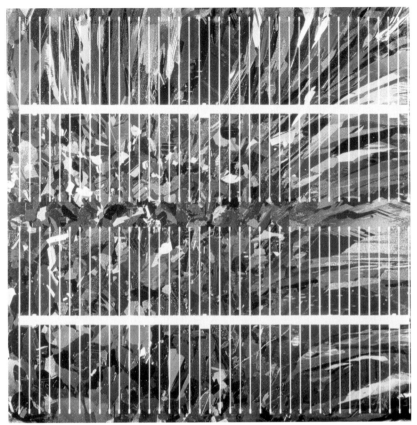

This is a close-up look at a photovoltaic (PV) cell, which uses crystals to convert sunlight into electrical energy.

when the Sun's rays fall on these crystals, some electrons break free. The loose electrons can be directed through an electrical circuit. The resulting current can be used to power lightbulbs, appliances, or anything else that runs on electricity. As long as the Sun shines, a PV device will continue to generate power.

There are countless uses for PV technology. Tiny PV panels are commonly used in small devices,

The International Space Station depends on rows of PV panels to supply all of its energy needs.

such as calculators and watches. Larger PV panels can provide backup power for traffic signals and other electronics. PV devices can also generate energy for objects that will be placed in remote, hard-to-service areas. Buoys far at sea, for example, are equipped with PV-powered sensors. Space satellites depend on PV panels for all of their power needs.

Homeowners can benefit from PV technology by placing solar panels on their roofs. The panels are usually mounted on the southern side of the roof, and they are carefully angled to catch the maximum amount of sunlight. Once installed, these panels pump electricity directly into the house below, thus reducing the amount of "grid" power (electricity provided by a utility company) a homeowner must purchase.

For consumers today, PV devices are one of the most practical ways to capture solar energy. Homeowners around the world are taking advantage of this technology. In early 2005, in fact, industry experts claimed that consumer demand was much greater than the supply of PV devices. Factories are expected to step up their production to meet this demand. Experts also believe PV technology will improve quickly as the market grows. As both of these changes occur, it may get easier and more practical for people everywhere to convert their homes to solar power.

chapter three

Putting Solar Power to Work

The techniques for capturing solar energy and changing it into usable power are very young. It has been only in the past two decades or so that these technologies have become widely available. But in this short time, it has become clear that solar power can be incredibly useful. People today are finding many ways to put sunlight to work.

Pool Party

One of the most common uses of solar power today is for heating swimming pools. Solar pool-heating systems include several large roof-mounted solar panels. The panels are dark, since dark colors absorb more heat than light colors, and they are angled to catch the maximum amount of sunlight. On a sunny day, these panels get very hot. Cold water from a swimming pool is pumped up to the roof and through the hot panels. When the water returns to the pool, it carries some of the Sun's heat with it.

Installing a solar pool-heating system is not cheap. For most homes, the price ranges from about $3,000 to $5,000, depending on the size of the pool. After the system has been installed, however, there are no additional costs. Throughout the system's fifteen- to twenty-year lifetime, the Sun heats the

Large solar panels mounted on the roof of a house in Phoenix, Arizona, heat the pool to a comfortable temperature.

pool for free. In comparison, electric pool heaters cost anywhere from $2,500 to $5,500 to install. And after installation, these units can use thousands of dollars' worth of electricity in a single year. So for homeowners in sunny areas, solar heating is not just environmentally friendly, it may also be the cheapest way to warm their water.

Solar heating is practical for more than just homeowners. It is proving to be useful for commercial facilities as well. The 1-million-gallon (3,785,411-liter) swimming pool built for the 1996 Olympic games in Atlanta, Georgia, is heated by the sun. The heat comes from a group of solar panels that covers more than 10,000 square feet (929 sq m). The building's owners estimate that this system is reducing their electric bills by more than $12,000 per year.

Electricity for Remote Areas

High electric bills, of course, are not a concern for the estimated 2 billion people who do not have access to electricity. Many of these people live in rural areas that may never be connected to a power grid. For remote families and communities like these, PV panels can generate enough electricity to power lightbulbs, pump water from wells, run small appliances and computers, and generally make life easier.

PV power forever changed the life of one resident of rural Hogan, Arizona. Helen Nez Sage had lived without electricity her entire life. To keep her family's food from spoiling, Sage made several trips per week to a store dozens of miles away to buy ice. Then, in 2000, Sage installed a solar-powered refrigerator in her home. The refrigerator gets the electricity it needs from PV panels mounted on Sage's roof. Today, the rest of Sage's home is still powerless, but food stays fresh and cold.

On a broader scale, PV is being used to bring power to villages in the developing countries of Africa, Asia, and South America. One of the largest projects undertaken so far has brought electricity to three entire villages in Nigeria's Jigawa state.

A home in a remote village in Brazil draws power from a solar panel installed by the Brazilian government.

A man holds up one of the panels from the solar energy system that will supply all of the energy needs of this Texas home.

Run by a charitable organization called the Solar Electric Light Fund (SELF), this project today is turning the Sun's rays into electric light, refrigeration, water pumping, computer access, and much more for 7,500 villagers. Many of the villages' new electrical devices, including water pumps and streetlights, use built-in PV panels to create their own electricity. Other electrical devices, such as lights and refrigerators inside hospitals and other buildings, draw their energy from large PV systems on top of buildings. Battery banks store extra electricity during the daytime so the systems can work at night or even during bad weather.

Because the Jigawa experiment has been so successful, SELF and the Nigerian government are currently planning to bring PV electricity to 30 additional villages. The ongoing Nigeria project, as well as SELF programs in China, India, Sri Lanka, Nepal, Vietnam, South Africa, and other countries, is proving that electricity provided by PV devices is a reliable, affordable, and economic source of power for rural households.

Built-In Power

Traditional PV panels are ideal for creating electricity in remote areas. There is plenty of room, so the panels can be mounted on poles wherever it is convenient. But in more developed areas, these panels are not always practical. They are bulky and heavy, and many buildings do not have a good place to mount them. Plus, many homeowners think PV panels are ugly. To overcome these problems, scientists have developed new types of PV devices that will blend into the design of just about any structure.

Roof shingles with a thin PV coating are one such product. PV shingles look just like regular shingles, but they behave in a very different way. From the moment they are installed, PV shingles produce a steady flow of electricity. In good conditions, they can generate enough power to pay for themselves in decreased power bills. Some users even make a profit from their solar roofs. Homeowners in England, for example, have reported that the solar shingles on their roofs generate more power in a year than they need to run their houses.

Shingles are not the only PV building products on the market. Tiles, aluminum siding, and other materials can also be turned into collectors for solar energy. They do this with the help of a thin PV film that can be molded onto any surface. The film does not generate as much electricity as traditional PV panels do, but for many people, the convenience of this technology makes up for the loss of efficiency.

Solar Pioneers

Like any new technology, solar power has a great deal of potential that has not been widely tapped. Scientists and organizations around the world are working to make the most of existing technologies and to invent new ones. By doing so, they are pushing the limits of humankind's knowledge about solar power.

One solar "pioneer" is radio station KTAO 101.9 FM near Taos, New Mexico. Since 1991, the station's transmitter has drawn every bit of its power from the Sun. The transmitter is equipped with 140 PV panels. The panels absorb New Mexico's hot sunshine during daytime hours and store it in a huge battery bank. At night, the transmitter pulls energy from the batteries so it can keep pumping

Solar-powered cars speed along the track during an eight-hour solar car race in Japan.

music out to its listeners. According to station officials, the system has performed flawlessly since the day it went online. KTAO's success proves that it is possible for a business to use solar power — and only solar power—as its energy source.

Another group of solar pioneers gathers every other July to compete in the North American Solar Challenge (NASC), formerly called the American Solar Challenge. The NASC is a competition to design, build, and race solar-powered cars across 2,500 miles (4,023km) of varied terrain, under changing weather conditions. Event organizers hope that the NASC will promote a greater understanding of solar energy technology, its environmental benefits, and its promise for the future. Someday the event may have a practical effect, too, if the technologies developed for NASC cars turn out to have commercial uses.

KTAO, the NASC, and other solar pioneers are attempting to show people that solar power really works. When people see with their own eyes how practical this energy source can be, they may be much more likely to use it in their homes and businesses.

chapter Four

Challenges to Overcome

Sunlight is free, it is everywhere, and it will never run out as long as the Sun continues to shine. After the manufacturing stage, solar power is also emission-free. For these reasons, solar energy might seem to be the perfect power source. But collecting and distributing solar energy is not easy. There are many challenges to overcome before solar energy can be a practical alternative to fossil fuels.

Solar Plants Are Expensive

Solar energy may be free, but collecting it is not. Right now, the biggest problem with solar power is the cost of producing it. Expensive concentrating solar power (CSP) plants must be built before large amounts of solar energy can be gathered.

31

The world's first solar power plant, the Solar One project in California, was very costly to build and maintain.

How expensive are CSP plants? Solar One, the world's first solar power plant, cost about $144 million to build and another $13 million to operate over its seven-year lifetime. In the early 1990s, Solar One was converted into Solar Two at an additional cost of about $40 million. So together, the two projects cost nearly $200 million. The price tags of other, more recent projects also top the $100-million mark.

Investors would not mind spending a lot of money to build a solar power plant if they thought they could make a lot of money in return. But solar power plants do not compare well to fossil fuel–run power plants in terms of profit. Today, electricity generated by solar power plants costs three to four times as much as traditional electricity, so solar electric power does not make sense on a dollars-and-cents basis alone.

Many people still believe in the future of solar power plants. They feel that costs will come down when technology improves and more plants are built. They also think it is important to be ready for the day when fossil fuels start to dwindle. For these reasons, solar power plants are springing up around the world. One large power tower, Solar Tres, is already operating in Spain. Trough systems are operating in California and Israel. And an enormous power tower is in the development stages in Australia. If the Australian Solar Tower is built, it is expected to produce enough electricity to run 200,000 households.

Home Systems Are Expensive

One of the greatest benefits of solar power is that it can be generated by individuals as well as by power plants. Anyone who is willing to install solar devices on his or her home can capture the Sun's energy and put it to use. By heating a home's water, air, and swimming pool with solar power, a homeowner spends less money on commercially produced electricity. Using PV panels to supply some of a home's power reduces the electric bill even more.

But it is still very expensive to install such a system, and the savings are not always great. It can cost more than $20,000 to install a full PV

The Dutch government helped the owners of these homes to pay for the installation of solar panels on the roof.

system on a home. Even under ideal conditions, it is unlikely that the system will save a homeowner that much money during its lifetime. Because the costs outweigh the benefits, there is not much incentive for consumers to install solar systems on their homes.

Despite the cost, thousands of people have invested in solar power for their homes. Most people, however, will not spend money on solar power devices until the rewards are greater than the expenses.

It Depends on the Sun

Another concern is that solar power is not very dependable. It does not work at night, and it works poorly under shadows or in cloudy conditions. A long rainy spell can stop solar plants and panels from creating electricity, and gray winter weather that lingers for months on end can have the same effect. Under conditions like these, an expensive solar power system can be nearly useless for days or weeks at a time.

It is not practical for businesses and homes to go without power when conditions prevent their solar devices from working, so most solar-powered buildings are connected to public utility lines. This lets them use regular electricity if they need to. Many solar systems also include batteries that store

A California man shows off the batteries that store solar energy collected from the PV system on the roof of his home.

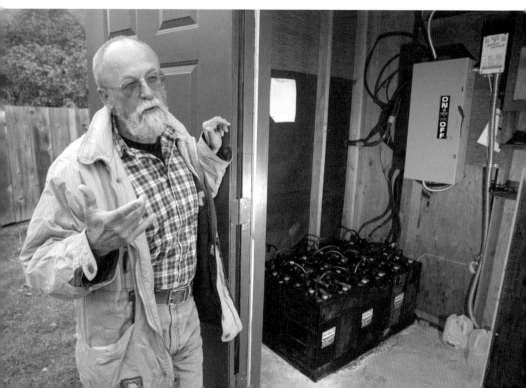

extra power during sunny times and release it at night or when conditions are otherwise poor. This stored power is helpful. But unless a home or business has an unusually large and expensive solar system, there is typically not enough stored power to meet all of a building's electricity needs.

Many people wonder why they should bother with solar power systems when they will still need to buy much or even most of their electricity from public utilities. This attitude is one more obstacle that solar power must address.

Overcoming the Problems

Not much can be done about the weather. But something *can* be done about the cost of solar power. Organizations around the world are working to make PV and other forms of solar technology easier on consumers' wallets.

Some governments are playing an important role in this effort by helping people to pay for solar power systems. In California, for example, homeowners and businesses pay only about half the cost of a system. The state picks up the rest of the tab. In New Jersey, the government pays for up to 70 percent of a solar installation.

Homeowners in Germany and Japan also get 70 percent. South Korea, Spain, Italy, China, and many other countries offer smaller but still important incentives. These funding programs can make solar

With their home disconnected from utility lines, this California couple relies entirely on solar power for their energy needs.

In the future, sustainable energy sources like solar power will likely become increasingly important and cost-effective.

power affordable for people who cannot or will not pay the entire bill.

In some areas, there is an extra benefit for consumers and businesses that install **grid-tied systems**. A grid-tied system produces solar electricity but is also connected to public utility lines.

Homes and businesses that are "on the grid" can sell any extra electricity they produce to their local utility companies. During the hot summer months, when solar energy is most intense, a grid-tied solar home may produce and sell enough power to pay its entire electric bill.

Industry observers predict that governments will stop paying for solar power soon. By the time this happens, however, solar technology could cost much less than it does today. One example of falling prices can be seen with PV panels, which are only half as expensive today as they were in the early 1990s. And prices could continue to fall as technologies improve.

No one can predict what the future holds. But it seems likely that solar power will get cheaper and fossil fuels will get more expensive. As this happens, solar technologies may become more and more attractive to people everywhere. Someday, not too long from now, solar power plants may be commonplace, and it might be hard to find a home or a business without a few solar panels on its roof.

Glossary

active: A type of solar heating system that uses mechanical devices to collect, store, or transfer the Sun's energy.

concentrating solar power: A device that uses mirrors to focus sunlight on a central point and heat a collecting agent.

condenses: When a vapor changes to a liquid.

dish system: A concentrating solar power device that uses bowl-shaped mirrors to reflect sunlight onto heat-powered engines.

emissions: Smoke, gases, or other substances that are discharged into the air.

fossil fuels: Fuels (including coal, oil, and natural gas) that are formed in the earth from plant or animal remains.

grid-tied systems: Solar power systems that are connected to public utility lines.

nonrenewable resource: A resource that is used up faster than it can be replaced.

nuclear fusion: The joining of two atoms.

nuclei (singular nucleus): Particles or groups of particles at the centers of atoms.

passive: A type of solar heating system that does not have any mechanical parts.

photovoltaic device: A device that converts sunlight directly into electricity. PV devices contain crystals that produce an electric current when exposed to sunlight.

power tower: The oldest type of concentrating solar power device. Computer-controlled mirrors surround and reflect sunlight onto a central tower.

renewable resource: A resource that is constantly replaced as it is being used.

solar energy: Energy generated by the Sun.

solar heating: Using the Sun's energy to heat homes.

solar power: Solar energy that has been collected and put to use.

trough system: A concentrating solar power device that uses rows of long, curved mirrors to reflect sunlight onto heat-collecting tubes.

For Further Exploration

Books

Jack Challoner, *Eyewitness: Energy*. New York: Dorling Kindersley, 2000. This book is an overview of many different types of energy, including their historic and modern uses.

Gary Chandler and Kevin Graham, *Alternative Energy Sources*. New York: Twenty-First Century, 1996. This book presents real-life examples of people and businesses that are finding new and unusual uses for alternative energy, including solar power.

Robert Gardner, *Science Project Ideas About the Sun*. Springfield, NJ: Enslow, 1997. Uses science experiments to illustrate the phases and patterns of the Sun, as well as its importance as an energy source.

Bonnie Juettner, *Energy*. San Diego, CA: KidHaven, 2005. Read about how the world uses and manages energy today, as well as some predictions about the future of energy usage.

Dana Meachen Rau, *Sun*. Minneapolis, MN: Compass Point, 2003. Describes the composition, surface features, and exploration of the Sun.

Web Sites

American Solar Challenge (www.american solarchallenge.org). Read all about the history and philosophy of the world's oldest solar race. Also includes up-to-the-minute information about the current race.

KTAO 101.9 FM (www.ktao.com). Learn more about groundbreaking solar station KTAO on the organization's Web site. A streaming audio link is included so visitors can listen to KTAO's music over the Internet.

Solar Electric Light Fund (www.self.org). SELF is bringing PV power to rural villages in the developing world. Read about SELF's past successes and current projects on this Web site.

Index

Picture credits

Cover: Getty Images
AP Wide Wolrd Photos, 25, 26
Alfred Pasieka/Photo Researchers, Inc., 19
Corel Corporation, 11, 38
© Da Silva Peter/CORBIS SYGMA, 35, 37
David Mack/Photo Researchers, Inc., 6
© Dean Conger/CORBIS, 23
Gregory MacNichol/Photo Researchers, Inc., 5
John Mead/Photo Researchers, Inc., 17
© Lowell Georgia/CORBIS, 32
Marti Bond/Photo Reseachers, Inc., 34
Maury Aaseng, 10, 14, 15
Photos.com, 20
© Reuters/CORBIS, 29

About the Author

Kris Hirschmann has written more than 100 books for children. She is the president of The Wordshop, a business that provides a variety of writing and editorial services. She holds a bachelor's degree in psychology from Dartmouth College in Hanover, New Hampshire. Hirschmann lives just outside Orlando, Florida, with her husband Michael and her daughters Nikki and Erika.